The
Very Worried
Sparrow

Meryl Doney

Illustrations by William Geldart

A LION PICTURE STORY
Oxford · Batavia · Sydney

When Jesus, who was the best of teachers, wanted to tell people something about God, he often chose examples from nature. In two of my favourite passages he talks about God as a caring father.

''Aren't five sparrows sold for two pennies? Yet not one sparrow is forgotten by God.''

''Look at the crows; they don't sow seeds or gather a harvest; they don't have store-rooms or barns; God feeds them! You are worth so much more than birds!''

I don't know whether animals and birds are aware of God (in their own way) or not. In this story I have imagined that they are.

There was once a Very Worried Sparrow. All the other birds looked up at the bright blue sky and sang for joy. But the Very Worried Sparrow hung his head, shut his beak tight and looked worried.

He had always worried, even when he was just a baby bird in the nest. His brothers and sisters kept saying, "Cheep, cheep, cheer up!"

But the Very Worried Sparrow only said, "Meep, meep, oh dear!"

When he began to grow, the first thing he worried about was food.

"Oh dear, oh dear!" he thought. "I'm so hungry, whatever am I going to eat?"

His brothers and sisters did not seem to worry at all. They just sat in the nest, looking up at the tree and the bright blue sky.

"It's because they don't think," he said to himself.

Suddenly there was a whirr of wings and his mother arrived with five fat juicy caterpillars in her beak.

"Cheep, cheep, cheep," went all the baby birds and she popped a caterpillar into each mouth.

Very soon all the baby birds were quite fat and their feathers had begun to grow.

One day Father bird said, "I think it is time you all learnt to fly."

"Cheep, cheep, hooray!" said the little birds – all except the Very Worried Sparrow.

He said, "Meep, meep, oh dear!" and looked more worried than ever.

The sparrows hopped out of the nest on to a big branch. They sat in a line bravely flapping their wings. One by one they set off.

"Wheeeeee, this is lovely," they called.

The Very Worried Sparrow hopped from one foot to the other.

"I'll never do it," he cheeped to himself. "Oh dear!"

He was so frightened, he lost his balance and toppled off the branch. He gulped, opened his little wings wide – and flew!

"There," said his mother as he landed beside her. "You can do it too."

As the spring days turned into warm summer the little
birds grew and grew. They learned to find caterpillars
among the green leaves and seeds on the brown earth.
Snip snap went their busy beaks.

All except the Very Worried Sparrow.

"It's such a big place out there," he thought. "I might
get lost, away from our nest. Meep, meep, oh dear!"

At dusk, when they were settling down for the night, Father sparrow gathered them all together, warm and snug in the nest. He began to tell them wonderful stories of long ago and far away:

of the Great Father who made the world and everything in it:

of how the day begins, and where the wind comes from, and all the little things that every creature knows.

The young birds listened with bright eyes. All except the Very Worried Sparrow. He was too worried to listen.

By midsummer the Very Worried Sparrow felt a bit braver. He set off from home, flying here and there, looking for food – and worrying about where to find it. The open fields looked a good place.

Suddenly a shadow rushed across the ground. The little sparrow felt his heart go "bump". Above him hovered the terrible Sparrowhawk.

He was too frightened even to worry! He crouched down small and still and waited.

There was a rush of wings in the air and the Sparrowhawk struck. When the sparrow opened his eyes he saw the hawk flying up and away. He held a small field-mouse in his great claw.

"Ooooooooh dear!" breathed the Very Worried Sparrow, feeling quite weak. "Oh dear, oh dear!"

As soon as he felt better he flew home as fast as his wings would carry him.

After that, the little sparrow looked more worried than ever. The autumn winds blew and the trees shed their leaves.

"Oh dear," thought the Very Worried Sparrow. "It's getting colder and colder. How shall I keep warm, and where am I going to find food to eat and water to drink?"

But he did. There was one little pond so sheltered that it didn't freeze. If he looked hard, he could still find seeds and berries in the hedges. And later on the children came and scattered bread on the snow.

Spring came at last and the snow melted away into the grass. The sparrows were very excited.

"It will soon be nesting time," they said, and began to look around for partners.

The girl sparrows giggled and whispered on the branches. The boy sparrows flew and swooped and showed off. Soon there were pairs of birds everywhere, searching for a safe place to build their nests.

Except for the Very Worried Sparrow.

"Oh dear!" he thought. "Now what shall I do? No one will want me for a mate."

Sadly he flew off by himself to the small apple tree at the far end of the garden.

But he found there was someone there already. It was another little sparrow and she looked very shy.

"Cheep," she said, in a small voice.

"Meep, meep," said the Very Worried Sparrow, suddenly looking more hopeful.

"Will you be my mate?" he asked, all in a rush.

"Oh, yes," said the shy little sparrow – and she smiled at him.

At first, the sparrow and his mate were very happy. But soon the Very Worried Sparrow started to worry again.

"Where shall we build our nest?" he thought. "The others have taken the best places."

The shy little sparrow flew back to the small apple tree at the far end of the garden.

"Look," she chirped, "no one has started to build here yet and it's very quiet and safe."

The apple blossom fell and new green leaves hid the nest from sight. Before long the shy little sparrow was sitting on the nest, looking very proud. Under her warm feathers were five beautiful eggs.

But the Very Worried Sparrow was looking very, very . . . worried.

"Meep, meep, oh dear!" he chirped. "I hope my eggs are safe. A cat might come. Or a hawk! The tree might fall. And how shall I feed the babies?"

"Roo, cooooo. What's the matter?" asked a gentle voice. It was a turtle-dove, with soft feathers and a very kindly look in her eyes. "I've never seen a sparrow look so worried before."

"Well," said the sparrow, sighing, "there are such a lot of things to worry about." And a big tear rolled down his beak and splashed on to his claw.

"Roo, cooooo," called the dove gently. "Don't you know about the Great Father who made us all? Haven't you been listening to the stories of long ago and far away?"

"Well no," sniffed the sparrow. "I was too worried to listen."

"Well," said the dove, "When you were a baby bird, didn't you always have food?"

"Why yes," said the sparrow.

"And when you learnt to fly, you didn't get hurt."

"No, I didn't," said the sparrow, thinking back.

"What about the Sparrowhawk?" the dove cooed gently. "Your time had not yet come, had it?"

"I suppose not," said the sparrow.

"And your food and water, your mate and your nest, and those beautiful eggs, they all came in good time, didn't they?"

"Yes, yes, they did!" chirped the sparrow, beginning to look a little happier.

"Will you come home with me please?" he said to the dove. "Come and tell us more. I promise I will listen this time."

And so the dove flew to the little apple tree at the far end of the garden and perched on the branch next to the nest. As the sun set slowly over the hill and all the birds were settling for sleep, the dove told the sparrows the stories of long ago and far away:

> of the Great Father who made the world and everything in it;
> of how the day begins, and where the wind comes from, and all the little things that every creature knows.

She spoke of the seasons and the years, of how things grow and new life comes. She told how the Great Father knows each creature and its time on the earth.

Next day, when the sun rose, everything looked
sparkling new in the morning light. The flowers opened
their faces to the sun and all the birds were singing.

There was a little noise from the nest.

"Tock, tock, tock," went one of the eggs. "Tock, tock,
tock!"

"It's our babies," cried the shy little sparrow excitedly.
"Today is the day they will hatch."

Then the Very Worried Sparrow . . . smiled.

He looked just as happy as his mate.

"I can't wait to see them," he said. "We can feed them
and watch them grow and teach them to fly. There are so
many things to do. And I want to tell them about the Great
Father who made the world and everything in it and who
knows each sparrow. Then they won't have to worry for a
single day."

And he flapped his wings and sang for joy with all the
other birds.

"Cheep, cheep," he sang. "Cheep, cheep, cheep,"
– loud enough to burst with happiness.

Text copyright © 1991 Meryl Doney
Illustrations copyright © 1991 William Geldart

Published by
Lion Publishing plc
Sandy Lane West, Oxford, England
ISBN 0 7459 1919 7
Lion Publishing Corporation
1705 Hubbard Avenue, Batavia, Illinois 60510, USA
ISBN 0 7459 1919 7
Albatross Books Pty Ltd
PO Box 320, Sutherland, NSW 2232, Australia
ISBN 0 7324 0231 X

First edition 1978
This revised and re-illustrated edition first published 1991

British Library Cataloguing in Publication Data
Doney, Meryl
    The very worried sparrow.
    I. Title   II. Geldart, William, *1936–*
    823.914 [J]
    ISBN 0 7459 1919 7

Library of Congress Cataloging in Publication Data
Doney, Meryl, 1942–
    The very worried Sparrow / by Meryl Doney ; illustrated by William
    Geldart.
    ISBN 0 7459 1919 7
    [1. Worry—Fiction.   2. Sparrows—Fiction.   3. Christian life—
    Fiction.]   I. Geldart, William, ill.   II. Title.
    PZ7.D7165Ve   1991
    [E]—dc20

Printed and bound in Singapore